Willa the Wonderful

Written and illustrated by **Susan Milord**

Houghton Mifflin Company
Boston

www.houghtonmifflinbooks.com

The text of this book is set in Stone Serif.
The illustrations are acrylic ink, watercolor, and colored pencil.

Library of Congress Cataloging-in-Publication Data

Milord, Susan.
Willa the wonderful / written and illustrated by Susan Milord.
p. cm.
Summary: When Willa announces her career goal to be a fairy princess,
her family and friends are skeptical until the day she makes a real-life rescue.
ISBN 0-618-27522-3 (hardcover)
[1. Fairies—Fiction. 2. Princesses—Fiction. 3. Schools—Fiction.
4. Rescues—Fiction.] I. Title.
PZ7.M6445 Wi 2003
[E]—dc21
2002011672

Printed in Singapore
TWP 10 9 8 7 6 5 4 3 2

For Bob the Believer

When Mr. Lane asked everyone in class
to write a report on a favorite career,
Willa grinned.
She knew exactly what she wanted to
be when she grew up.

Willa wanted to be a fairy princess.

"I don't think that's what Mr. Lane had in mind," her father said.

"I've never met a fairy princess," her mother remarked. "What exactly do they do?"

"Lots of things," Willa replied. "But mostly they make good things happen. You'll see."

Willa already knew quite a bit about fairy princesses.
She knew all about the frilly dresses they wore.
She knew about fairy dust and magic wands.
Writing her report would be a cinch.

She searched in her Dress-Up box for something to wear.
She found an old tutu.

She cut out lots and lots of stars.

She made a pair of wings.

She selected the perfect wand.

She filled a sack with fairy dust.

"Are you sure you have everything you need?"
Willa's father wondered.
   "Are you ready?" her mother asked.
Willa nodded. Like all good fairy princesses,
Willa was ready for anything.

The bus driver shook his head when he saw Willa.
"Sorry," he said. "No flying creatures allowed on my bus."
Willa's wings rode in the front of the bus.
The rest of her rode in the back.

Mr. Lane listened while Willa explained that
she was learning about her job firsthand.
That didn't keep him from suggesting, three
times, that Willa put her wand away.
It disappeared into his desk drawer.

Ms. Bremner wasn't sure Willa should wear her fairy princess outfit for gym.

"Just watch," Willa told her. "My leaps will be higher than ever."

Luckily, Ms. Bremner was looking the other way when Willa landed.

At recess, Willa and her best friend, Jenny, were chased by a monster.

"Help! It's getting closer!" Jenny cried, barely inches ahead of Sherman, her little brother.

"I'll make us invisible," Willa said. "Then It won't be able to catch us!"

Willa mumbled a few magic words.
She tossed some fairy dust into the air.

"Hey!" cried Jenny. "Why did you throw
dirt in my hair?"

"You don't know much about fairy dust, do you?"
Willa snorted.

"I know one thing," Jenny said. "You've taken
this fairy princess thing too far."
Jenny played with Doreen the rest of recess.

Being a fairy princess was turning out to be harder
than Willa had imagined.
She'd made only bad things happen all day.
She'd even managed to lose her best friend.

The whispers and sideways glances finally got to her. During spelling, she blurted out, "I may not be much of a fairy princess yet, but just wait. I've got what it takes. I'll show you!"

Mr. Lane showed Willa to the Thinking Chair. She stayed there until the bell rang.

Willa kept on thinking all the way home.
Maybe she'd been wrong.
Maybe being a fairy princess wasn't the job for her.

She was deep in thought when Sherman
darted in front of her.
He was chasing a ball, and it was headed
for the street.

It was a lucky thing that a little red wagon
blocked Sherman's way.

It was not such a lucky thing that the wagon and Sherman collided.

The wagon began to roll down the hill. Waving her magic wand, Willa flew after it.

She dodged a planter of petunias,

leapt over a toy truck,

and narrowly avoided a trash can.

She grabbed the wagon just in time.

Willa sprinkled fairy dust on Sherman. She recited a magic spell and waved her wand some more.

It worked. Sherman was okay.

The next morning, Willa wondered why Jenny
wasn't on the bus.

She wondered why she wasn't on the playground.

Mr. Lane had already taken attendance when Jenny walked into the classroom.

She was followed by Sherman and their parents, who were carrying a cake with the words

Thank you
Willa

written in pink icing on the top.

Willa was even more surprised when her own parents came into the classroom.

"News travels fast," Willa's mother explained.

"Almost as fast as the fairy princess who made that daring rescue," her father said.

"That was no fairy princess, Daddy—that was *me!*" Willa insisted.

"Of course it was," agreed her parents.

While everyone snacked on cake,
Willa and Sherman told the class
all about their adventure.

"I guess you had what it takes to be a fairy princess
all along," Jenny said. "Except for maybe one thing."
She placed a gold crown on Willa's head.
Willa grinned her biggest grin.

"You sure showed us, Willa. Good job," Mr. Lane said.
  "Actually," Willa corrected him, "being a fairy
princess is a *wonderful* job."

The Life
of a
Fairy Princess

by
Willa

Northport-East Northport Public Library

To view your patron record from a computer, click on
the Library's homepage: **www.nenpl.org**

You may:
- request an item be placed on hold
- renew an item that is overdue
- view titles and due dates checked out on your card
- view your own outstanding fines

185 Larkfield Road
East Northport, NY 11731
631-261-2313